Ludwig Gruner, Vittore Ottolini, Friedrich Lose

The Terra-Cotta Architecture of North Italy

XIIth-XVth centuries - pourtrayed as examples for imitation in other countries

Ludwig Gruner, Vittore Ottolini, Friedrich Lose

The Terra-Cotta Architecture of North Italy
XIIth-XVth centuries - pourtrayed as examples for imitation in other countries

ISBN/EAN: 9783337614157

Printed in Europe, USA, Canada, Australia, Japan

Cover: Foto ©Andreas Hilbeck / pixelio.de

More available books at **www.hansebooks.com**

THE

TERRA-COTTA ARCHITECTURE

OF

NORTH ITALY

(XIITH–XVTH CENTURIES)

POURTRAYED AS EXAMPLES FOR IMITATION IN OTHER COUNTRIES

FROM CAREFUL DRAWINGS AND RESTORATIONS BY

FEDERIGO LOSE

FORTY-EIGHT ILLUSTRATIONS ENGRAVED AND PRINTED IN COLOURS, WITH WOODCUT SECTIONS, MOULDINGS, ETC
AND DESCRIPTIVE TEXT BY V. OTTOLINI AND F. LOSE

EDITED BY

LEWIS GRUNER

LONDON
JOHN MURRAY, ALBEMARLE STREET
1867

To

HER ROYAL HIGHNESS

VICTORIA ADELAIDE MARY LOUISA

CROWN PRINCESS OF PRUSSIA

PRINCESS ROYAL OF GREAT BRITAIN AND IRELAND

&c. &c.

THIS WORK

EXHIBITING SPECIMENS OF TERRA-COTTA BUILDINGS IN UPPER ITALY

IS

BY HER ROYAL HIGHNESS'S SPECIAL PERMISSION

Dedicated

BY

HER ROYAL HIGHNESS'S OBLIGED AND HUMBLE SERVANT

LEWIS GRUNER

LIST OF PLATES.

PLATE   PAGE.

1. CHURCH OF SANTA EUFEMIA, AT PAVIA .   . 11

2. SAN PIETRO IN CIEL D'ORO, AT PAVIA   13

3. ELEVATION AND SECTION OF THE CERTOSA, CHIARAVALLE .   . 15

4. CENTRAL PORTION OF SPIRE OF CERTOSA, CHIARAVALLE .   . 15

5. MIDDLE PORTION OF CAMPANILE DI SAN GOTTARDO, AT MILAN .   21

6. UPPER PORTION OF THE SAME   21

7. FRONT OF CHURCH OF SANTA MARIA DEL CARMINE, PAVIA   27

8. PART OF FAÇADE OF SANTA MARIA DEL CARMINE   . 27

9. PART OF CENTRAL WINDOW OF THE SAME   27

10. WINDOW IN FAÇADE OF THE SAME .   27

11. CAMPANILE OF THE CHURCH OF THE CARMINE   27

12. PART OF THE FAÇADE OF SAN FRANCESCO, PAVIA   . 31

13. PLAN, ELEVATION, AND SECTION OF THE PALACE OR CASTLE OF GIAN-
        GALEAZZO VISCONTI, AT PAVIA 33

14. ONE OF THE SIDES OF THE COURTYARD (SEE PLAN A, PL. 13)   33

a

PLATE		PAGE
15.	ANOTHER SIDE OF THE SAME COURTYARD (SEE PLAN B, PL. 13)	33
16.	FAÇADE OF THE CATHEDRAL OF CREMA	37
17.	UPPER CENTRAL WINDOW IN THE FAÇADE OF THE CATHEDRAL OF CREMA	37
18.	UPPER WINDOW OF THE CATHEDRAL, CREMA, LEFT SIDE	37
19.	UPPER WINDOW OF THE SAME, RIGHT SIDE	37
20.	LOWER WINDOW FROM THE SAME FAÇADE	37
21.	DETAILS OF FAÇADE OF THE CATHEDRAL OF CREMA	37
22.	OTHER DETAILS OF THE SAME	37
23.	THE CAMPANILE OF THE CATHEDRAL OF CREMA	41
24.	UPPER PART OF THE CAMPANILE OF THE CATHEDRAL OF CREMA	41
25.	DETAILS FROM THE CAMPANILE, CREMA	41
26.	FAÇADE OF SS. FERMO AND RUSTICO, AT CARAVAGGIO	43
27.	UPPER PORTION OF THE FAÇADE OF SS. FERMO AND RUSTICO	43
28.	THE CAMPANILE OF SS. FERMO AND RUSTICO	45
29.	LATERAL APSE OF THE CERTOSA, NEAR PAVIA	47
30.	ARCADE FROM THE CLOISTERS OF THE CERTOSA, NEAR PAVIA	47
31.	ANOTHER ARCADE FROM THE SAME	47
32.	ANOTHER ARCADE FROM THE SAME	47
33.	VARIOUS SPIRES AND CHIMNEYS AND CLOCK TOWER OF THE CERTOSA	47

PLATE   PAGE

34. FRONT VIEW OF SANTA MARIA IN STRADA, MONZA .   53

35. PRINCIPAL ENTRANCE OF SANTA MARIA IN STRADA .   53

36. TWO WINDOWS AT THE SIDE OF THE CATHEDRAL OF MONZA .   55

37. VIEW OF SANTA MARIA DELLA CROCE, CALLED THE SANTUARIO DI CREMA (PHOTOGRAPH)   57

38. VIEW OF THE UPPER PORTION OF THE SANTUARIO, AT CREMA .   57

39. COURT IN A PRIVATE HOUSE, AT PAVIA .   59

40. UPPER PART OF A PRIVATE HOUSE, AT PAVIA .   61

41. PORTION OF A PALACE OF THE VISCONTI AND SFORZAS AT CUSAGO .   63

42. ELEVATION OF A HOUSE, AT PAVIA, NEAR THE HOSPITAL .   65

43. WINDOW IN A PRIVATE HOUSE, AT PAVIA   67

44. CASA ARCIMBOLDI, NOW BUSCA, NEAR MILAN .   69

45. (a) UPPER PART OF VILLA NEAR THE MADONNA DEL MONTE, VARESE; (b) SIMILAR DECORATION FROM VILLA UBALDO, SARONNO   71

46. WINDOW OF A CASINO DI CAMPAGNA   71

47. PORTION OF A PRIVATE HOUSE, AT BRESCIA   75

48. UPPER PORTION OF A CAMPANILE, AT PAVIA   77

INTRODUCTION.

—⟶⟩∘⟨⟵—

SKETCH OF THE HISTORY OF TERRA-COTTAS:

AND A BRIEF DESCRIPTION OF THE

BEST METHODS USED IN ITALY TO PRODUCE THEM.

S the object of the present work is entirely practical, it is by no means necessary to advance into the barren and boundless field of strictly scientific investigation in search of the origin of terra-cottas and of their special application as ornamental portions of buildings. Were anything further to be attempted, we feel that we should trench on the province of archæology, of ceramic art, and of potter's work, subjects entirely beyond the aims which we propose to carry out.

Nevertheless, to touch in passing upon some of the ideas most generally held as to terra-cotta, let us observe with D'Agincourt,[1] that ' soft clay being of all substances that which lies most ready to the hand of man, could not but be found most available for an infinite number of objects of first necessity.' And to this should be added the obvious consideration, that the first inhabitants of the earth, by kindling fire on a clayey soil, must have found that the under-lying clay becoming heated acquired hardness and cohesiveness; and it is natural that, pondering this most simple phenomenon, they should have rounded and hollowed in the middle a lump of clayey mire, using it at first to draw water or contain liquids, afterwards, having tempered it by fire, in cooking food.

[1] Recueil de Fragmens de Sculpture Antique en Terre-cuite. Paris, 1814.

B

Next, studying the history of terra-cottas under their aspect as ornamental details, not to speak of other facts which attest their use at a remote period, let us cite the words of Cicognara,[1] where he discourses of the origin of the sculptural art: 'Who knows how often and amid how many nations may not have happened that which was related in Corinth of the potter Dibutades of Sicyon, whose daughter traced on the wall the shadow of the face of her lover who was about to leave her; and the outline of whose shadow, filled with clay by the father, produced the first profile in bas-relief, and was baked in the furnace along with the tiles?'

Following the course of time we observe, with the distinguished Thomas Hope,[2] that 'the ancient Greeks seem everywhere in their mother country, and their different later colonies, to have found stone too plentifully to make great use of brick, though a few remains of terra-cotta cornices have been found even in Greece, as well as terra-cotta vases and bas-reliefs.

'The ancient Romans, wherever they found clay more abundant or easier to work than stone, used it plentifully, both in regular layers throughout the body of walls, as we do, and in an external reticulated coating, which has proved to be as durable as stone itself from the fineness of its texture and the firmness of its joints. Indeed, far from considering brick as a material fit only for the coarsest and most indispensable groundwork of architecture, they regarded it as equally adapted for all the elegances of ornamental form—all the details of rich architraves, capitals, friezes, cornices, and other embellishments. Sometimes it owed to the mould its various forms, and at others, as in the Amphitheatrum Castrense and the temple of the god Rediculus, to the chisel.

'In modern Rome, too, very great use was made of brick until a very late period. Of the grand Farnese palace, begun by Bramante and finished by Michael Angelo, the plain surfaces are of brick, so fine in its texture and so

---

[1] Storia della Scultura dal suo Risorgimento in Italia fino al secolo di Napoleone, ecc., tomo 1, p. 21, Venezia, 1813.

[2] This extract is from a MS. note by Hope, appended to his 'Historical Essay on Architecture,' and is also published in the Italian version of his work made by G. Imperatori, Milan, 1840.

neat in its joints, that by the superficial observer it is generally taken for stone. In the plains of Lombardy, where stone is rare, clay has, in buildings of importance, been moulded into forms so exquisite, as to have been raised into a material of value and dignity. In the ancient churches of Pavia, &c., it presents itself in all the delicate tracery of the Middle Ages; in the ' Ospitale Maggiore' and Castiglione palace, at Milan, it exhibits the arabesque and medallions of the Cinque-cento style. On this side of the Alps, clay has never been moulded into forms quite so elaborate; still, in the south of France, particularly at Toulouse, remarkable examples exist. Along the Rhone, carved tiles are formed into very elegant cornices and balustrades. In the north of Germany, in Brandenburg, Luneburg, Hanover, and the provinces bordering on the Baltic, brick and richly ornamented terra-cottas perform the part of stone, not only for the exterior but for the interior of churches, towers, halls, and private houses, even the lofty piers of cathedrals being moulded in clay. Even in England brick was, in former days, modelled and cast into artistic and ornamental forms. But, whether in consequence of the high duty imposed upon brick, and the consequent limitation as to size and shape, or from the influence of the contract system of building, the legal English brick has become by degrees the least durable and most unsightly in use in any country; and has hence produced that dislike to its colour and material, which proceeds, not from its intrinsic ugliness, but from association of the imagination with ideas of coarseness and meanness of construction.'

Lombardy is especially rich in ancient works of terra-cotta; so much so that Hope calls it 'the great country of brick.' Amongst the most ancient we will merely mention the crypts of the church of Lenno on the Lake of Como, where are still preserved various remains of colossal statues in terra-cotta of a close-grained and tough consistency, and which all appear to belong to the constructions of Christianity.

In Italy the art of terra-cotta attained its crowning development during the prevalence of the Renaissance style, as noble monuments, both sacred and profane, attest. Then were produced very fine and beautiful ornaments in terra-cotta, even at a cost not exceeding the resources of private persons; then was attained that seemly comeliness and that elegant exterior which are so powerful to diffuse good taste among the people. In that golden age of the art a wise sobriety was observed in the use of such ornaments, and a scrupulous care to apply them only where the style permitted them. From the most celebrated architects who flourished along with Luca della Robbia, that pre-eminent modeller in terra-cotta, down to the period of the Renaissance, ceramic ornament invariably entered into designs for buildings.

It was then in the fifteenth and sixteenth centuries that the art of terra-cotta most flourished; but when it passed into the hands of the so-called imitators of Michael Angelo, art overpassing the boundary line of beauty, lapsed into exaggeration, then the modest, severe, and delicate ornament in terra-cotta, refusing to lend itself to the contortions and scroll-work of the 'Barocco' style, fell suddenly into oblivion, and there remained until our own times.

To this rapid sketch of the history of terra-cottas we subjoin a word as to the best methods of producing them employed in Italy, which in that country have regained for this branch of industry its due importance.

Only a few years ago the art was revived in Milan by the sculptor Andrea Boni; and the Royal Lombardic Institute first gave him the encouragement of a silver medal, and afterwards rewarded him with one of gold.

To convey an adequate and detailed idea of the best method employed in Italy for building in terra-cotta, of the modes of drying the modelled objects, of their baking, and of other improvements, it will suffice to explain the system now carried out by Boni in his extensive and busy manufactory in Milan, a system of which the results were highly praised at the Great Exhibition in South Kensington Museum.[1]

He manufactures two sorts of ware; one calculated to resist atmospheric

---

[1] We derive these particulars from the reports of the Commission of the Royal Lombardic Institute of Sciences, Letters, and Arts (Collezione degli Atti delle solenni distribuzioni dei premj d' Industria fatte in Milano ed in Venezia dal 1853 al 1857, vol. viii. Milano, 1857), and from an account by Professor Magrini.

action and shocks, the other of less tenacity, but in grain and tone more resembling the ancient terra-cottas, and less costly than the former.

To produce the first sort, which in baking turns out almost ash-coloured, he employs a mixture of whitish clays of somewhat tough consistency, which are found in the neighbourhood of Maggiora, mixed with finely-powdered quartz.

The second sort, at present most in vogue, is composed of two parts of the above-named clays of Maggiora; four parts of rich and very ferruginous earth of a deep red hue, found in the territory of Lesmo; four parts of tougher earth, derived from Trezzo; and two parts of a sandy lime of finest grain, gathered in the commune of Ronco, which, as a disjunctive element, increases the porosity, and prevents the excessive cohesion of the pieces.

Plasticity and homogeneity of ingredients are the two conditions essential to the composition of any ceramic paste. Plasticity is the property of clays which contain only aluminum, silica, and a little oxide of iron; and depends in great measure on the water contained in the clay, which cannot be evaporated even by the drying power of 100 degrees.[1]

Clays, regarded even as hydrated silicates of aluminum, were at first supposed to owe their elasticity to the aluminum alone. But since this substance, whether already reduced to a gelatinous state, or kneaded long while in water, never furnishes a tenacious and plastic paste however pure silica may be mixed

---

[1] "All clays as they occur in nature are essentially *hydrated* silicates of alumina; and upon the presence of the water of *combination* depends their fictile or plastic property, that is, their capability of being moulded into vessels when mixed with water and kneaded to a pasty consistency. All clays contain *hygroscopic* water, which may be expelled at 100° C. without lessening their plasticity. When, however, clay is heated to redness, it loses not only its hygroscopic water, but also its water of combination, and, as a consequence, it ceases to be plastic. In this dehydrated state it cannot again directly *combine* with water and regain its plasticity. It may, indeed, *absorb* water with avidity; but not the smallest degree of plasticity is thereby restored. Pounded brick, for example, is dehydrated clay; and it may absorb a considerable quantity of water without regaining the slightest amount of plasticity.

If we compare different clays together in respect to elementary composition, we find the relation between the silica and alumina to be extremely variable; and, accordingly, the formulæ which have been proposed to express their rational constitution are very discordant. This is in great measure to be explained by the fact that, in many clays, a large proportion of silica exists uncombined either as sand, or in a much finer state of division. The grittiness of a clay is due to the presence of sand." Dr. Percy's 'Metallurgy and Fire Clays,' vol. i. p. 208.

c

with it in the very proportion in which it occurs in the composition of clays, we must admit that these possess some particular texture or molecular arrangement which the natural circumstances of their formation and, above all, time have imparted to the constituent parts; a texture which man has not as yet—so at least it seems to us—learned how to imitate completely.

Yet although plasticity be an all important condition of this manufacture, its excess entails grave inconvenience. Objects formed of over-plastic clays are dried unequally and with difficulty, which renders them liable to lose shape and crack. Such defects are developed at the stove, and in the furnace they increase further. Hence, as we mentioned, arises the necessity of introducing into the composition of the paste powdered quartz, calcareous earths, and sands, to diminish this excessive plasticity, increase porosity, and thus facilitate the expulsion of the water; which, although it serves merely to mix the materials and give them the needful softness, demands weighty consideration and precautions; because the wrought portions, however they may sometimes seem dry, never are absolutely free from water.

We have already observed that the liquid is strongly attracted by the clay, or, more strictly speaking, so combines with the clay as to require an intense heat for its total elimination. It has been stated that sandy substances make an easy channel for the water to pass from molecule to molecule, thus securing to all parts an equal density. Now, to the end that the desiccation of the largest pieces may be effected uniformly and without cracking, care must be taken to diminish the density at the centre; because, if the outside density did not exceed the inner, the evaporation of water must naturally proceed more slowly at the centre, the clays would from the first remain in an unavoidable state of lumpishness, and a separation of their molecules must ensue.

Rapid drying gives rise to another serious defect: the work becomes coated superficially with a dry thick crust impervious to internal moisture; and thus appears dry when only partially so. The result is that the imprisoned water, constrained in the furnace to evaporate by the high temperature, acquires an elastic force sufficient not only to crack the piece that contains it, but even to split it to fragments. This is the reason why Boni adheres to the system of applying the paste in small pieces to the moulds, and leaving spaces at intervals; thus endeavouring to obtain an equal, slow, and thorough expulsion of the water from the modelled paste. For this reason, having studied the proportions of the disjunctive materials, he finds it needful to protect his works from the direct and too forcible action of the wind, and to watch that they be always accessible to the steady and beneficial influence of heat and light.

Thus the pieces withdrawn from the moulds are dried in the calm open air, if small at the stove, if bulky at the furnace. To effect this, a large board is set up on an inclined plane, under which is fixed a vessel of sheet-iron to carry off the heated air and the products of that combustion which is regulated in the stove.

By these contrivances the large pieces are almost always preserved from cracking, because the paste, being of uniform substance throughout every atom of it, submits to the same conditions, and undergoes equally the shrinking process, the upper portions gravitating infallibly though lightly on the lower.

So soon as the moulded objects have attained the due degree of dryness, they are polished by hand and consigned to the furnace, where the burning is effected by means of combustibles calculated to emit flame.

The fireplace is fitted with a roof on which are arranged the pieces to be burnt; and the flames ascend amongst them by means of many apertures pierced in the roof itself; wherefore combustibles which burn with a long-sustained flame are to be chosen even though inferior in point of heat. In the Milanese workshops wood is the fuel preferred on economic grounds.

Yet all this care in drying and firing would fail to ensure solidity to the work, if the conditions essential for obtaining perfect homogeneity and compactness of the earths were not first observed. In ceramic pastes two kinds of homogeneity must be aimed at: one of parts, the other of masses. The first consists in equality of nature, uniformity of volume, invariableness of density, in each constituent of the paste; and is attained by working, by kneading, by sifting, finally by mixing the ingredients already finely pulverized. The second, and more important, results from an uniform blending of the dissolved earths; so that the inevitable modifications produced by desiccation and burning may affect alike every portion of the mass, which renders it highly advisable that, before moulding, the earths be subjected to much kneading with hands and feet.

A paste, not thoroughly homogeneous, fails to sustain equally in all parts the influence of heat. Hence neither judicious choice and just balance of ingredients, nor washings, grindings, mixings, slow desiccation, will suffice: to render the paste homogeneous, mastery of molecular forces must be secured. Homogeneity is a final result brought about by minute processes carried on through a lengthened period. It is therefore indispensable that vast dépôts be formed, where the excavated materials, before being reduced to a paste, may undergo at leisure atmospheric influences, and where large masses of the damp paste may remain for some years so as truly to rot, to give scope, that is, to the daily internal motions of the molecules themselves, before undergoing moulding or modelling, and being exposed to the action of fire.

On these conditions only can terra-cottas modelled in relief attain, from an industrial point of view, their perfection.

The way in which terra-cottas were introduced into walls was not unlike that commonly used for inserting stone, marble, corbels, and jambs of stone. It is evident that the general skeleton of the wall was first constructed, keeping some bricks protruding, so that afterwards the casts, figures, heads, cornices, and such like, might be introduced into the interstices left between brick and brick out of the redundant material beyond the substance of the wall itself. Such pieces, if flat or slightly salient, were fixed in simply with lime and plaster; at the most, for greater strength, hooks of iron or mere nails were used. Large blocks were secured in the same way as corbels or stone cornices: they took, · however, the precaution to hollow out by hand such figures as required to be fixed to the bricks that jutted beyond the wall-level ; sometimes also in order to lighten them, or to promote the uniform burning of large pieces, such as large heads and statues. The utmost care to strengthen them was bestowed on the first rows of cornices, and on such architectural members as had to sustain others ; these upper portions, on the contrary, being borne by the lower and fixed to the wall as best might be without any extreme care, but never made salient by excessive or abrupt protrusion. They are always graduated and pitched, so that rain-water may never flow down behind, but invariably along, their front. Here in Italy, through the sudden changes of temperature, frost will soon split the hardest marbles ; nevertheless, although these terra-cottas are not attached to the wall in a very elaborate fashion, yet in consequence of the builder's precautions to prevent water standing on them, they appear little injured by frost.

No better evidence can be produced of the uniform care employed in the kneading and burning of the clay, than the rarity of inequalities or discolorations to be discerned in it.

V. OTTOLINI.

Milan, January, 1867.

PLATE I.

As the present work aims at supplying architects and manufacturers, students and amateurs, with a series of specimens of terra-cotta, commencing with simple and proceeding to more elaborate forms, and gives examples from the remotest date down to the latest mediæval period, it seems well to devote our first plate to the representation of the apse of the Church of Santa Eufemia, Pavia, of which the architecture is both the oldest (I assign it to the eleventh century) and the simplest. Of this style, known throughout Italy as the Gothic-Lombard, the name seems to me incorrect and merely local. The style has its own exclusive characteristics, is referable to the dark ages and the mediæval period, and reached its full development merely in the valley of the Po; and as I hold the principles of this architectural school to have been imported from the East by Constantinopolitan (Byzantine) artists, then modified according to the fashion or fancy of the architects who established themselves here, and lastly cultivated and reduced to system by their disciples, so to my thinking this style should rather be named the Byzantine-Lombard. We know that the early Christians aimed at imparting to their churches and other buildings a character unlike that of the Pagan temples; and thus they evolved a system of architectural decoration which accorded with the religious ideas and gravely simple rites of those times; the Ecclesiastical services then observed in the valley of the Po (Lombardy) being fashioned according to the Greek model, of which a proof survives in the famous Ambrosian ritual; all which bears out my theory that this architectural style was based on notions imported from Greece in the Middle Ages.

It is usual in Italy to call the thirteenth and fourteenth centuries the epoch of the Renaissance; a term applied in France to the sixteenth century. It seems to me, however, that no defined age of renaissance can be indicated; a point illustrated by our present series of plates, which reproduce in obvious gradations of progress a succession of buildings from the eleventh to the fifteenth century. Still we cannot avoid recognising a distinct period of decay during the ascendancy of that so-called barocco or rococo school, which flourished in the sixteenth and throughout the seventeenth centuries.

Our first plate represents a style of architecture of the utmost imaginable simplicity, which yet pleases the eye by varied lines of different heights and thicknesses, whether intersecting, straight, or curved; and produces an outline, pictorial and justly pyramidal in its proportion. Monotony also is avoided, and the general design is rendered more intelligible by the little interruptions of alternating bricks and stones.

Since the classic architecture of Greece and Rome was after all but of man's invention, the veneration in which it is held by many architects who accept the precepts of Vitruvius and Vignola as gospel appears to me exaggerated. When I behold an architecture as logical and rational as this of ours I respect it in its simplicity no less than the simple Doric order of Vignola; indeed, whilst as a whole it looks well and is impressed with the venerable character suitable to a religious edifice, it does in fact, under circumstances apparently far less favourable, affect the soul far more deeply.

Behind the choir of Santa Euphemia lies an ascending path little more than a yard wide, along which the edifice is gradually approached and seen point by point, each successive point coming into view and vanishing in its turn: the perspective lines appear peculiarly oblique and inclined; the cupola is altogether hidden, yet the effect on the mind is not hereby lessened but rather heightened into sombre awe and an inexpressible religiousness. That interminable array of bricks, those arches which sustain the cornices, appear grand when seen few at a time and near: there arises an expectation of vastness, of further portions yet to come of the entire edifice; and as one pursues this narrow path surprise augments, and the building seems to exceed its actual standard of grandeur and complication. Those edifices are to be admired which show forth their appropriate character equally when seen close at hand and from afar.

F. LOSE.

San Pietro in Ciela d'Oro at Pavia

PLATE 2.

SAN PIETRO IN CIEL D'ORO, PAVIA.

THE building of this church is attributed to the Lombard king Agilulph in 604. Chroniclers however, copying one from the other, agree in asserting that King Liutprand, in 723, translated thither from Sardinia, with splendid pomp and at a heavy expense, the body of S. Augustine, and deposited it in the magnificent white marble shrine which now adorns the cathedral of Pavia, whither it was transported 1799. In San Pietro in Ciel d'Oro was also placed the urn of Severinus Boëthius, put to death by Theodoric at no great distance from this spot, which urn was likewise removed to the above-named cathedral.

The vault of the principal apse of this basilica was gilded after the fashion of the Byzantine artists; and hence was derived the name of San Pietro in Ciel d'Oro (S. Peter in a Canopy or Heaven of Gold). The body of this church was ceiled with timber, and portions of the ancient beams yet remain. The vaulting was probably constructed in the fourteenth century, at which period most of the ancient unfinished basilicas were vaulted.

Selvatico in his *Storia dell' Estetica* mentions that Liutprand caused this church to be magnificently decorated, in order to profit by the ability of the numerous Byzantine artists, who had left their native land to escape the wrath of Leo the Isaurian during the rage of the Iconoclasts.

We have narrated what legends and chroniclers tell us concerning this basilica; yet there survives no historic record of aught that befel it from its foundation down to the year 1132, when it was consecrated by Pope Innocent II. This fact may raise a doubt whether the church was reconstructed in the eleventh century, or at the beginning of the twelfth, an opinion well worthy of consideration.

The ancient basilica of San Pietro in Ciel d'Oro is mentioned by Dante, by Boccaccio, and by Vasari.[1] We cannot furnish any account of the interior decorations of this basilica, since ignorance and superstition destroyed all traces of them, chipping away and erasing the very sculptured capitals that adorned its piers, because they were supposed to be heathen symbols. It is certain, however, that there were fine moulded sculptures; and that, originally, the whole, even to the relief of the capitals, was painted. It possesses an ancient doorway, which, together with the string-courses of the windows, and the cross vaulting (' croce vuota '), appear to be of a calcareous stone less compact than sandstone. Here and there are scattered various holy-water basins differing in size and colour. Around the octangular cupola runs a loggia or gallery for use on a small scale, supported by the usual small columns.

Of old there must undoubtedly have stood, in front of the building, a vestibule or *narthex*, as was the case with all important basilicas. This is proved by the small columns, which jut out beside the front buttresses, adorned with capitals, and supporting an arch of bricks built together, not to speak of the trace of an arch traversing the same loggia, and still visible on the outside of the buttress, which contains the staircase by which you ascend to the small loggia of the front.

In the fourteenth century this church was leaded over to render the roof water-tight. Some years ago an ignorant bishop, fearful least the church might fall, caused the right aisle to be pulled down, and ceased from the work of destruction only when the master-mason represented to him how vain it was to squander money on knocking down walls which time itself had failed to shake. Yet still from what remains may be discerned how the wear and tear of years have told less upon the terra-cotta than upon the stone here and there built in with it, although the climate of Pavia, even when compared with the rest of Lombardy, is specially damp and foggy.   O.

---

[1] Dante, alluding to the soul of Boëthius, writes :

' Lo corpo ond' ella fu cacciata, giace
   Giuso in Cieldauro, et essa da martiro
   E da esilio venne a questa pace.'

' That body whence her violent decease
She made, Cieldauro covers ; and she ran
From pangs and exile into th' endless peace.'
     Paradise, ex. Cayley's translation.

And so Boccaccio in the tenth day of the ' Decameron : ' 'Already in the church of San Pietro in Ciel d'Oro, at Pavia, had been deposited Messer Torello,' &c. Vasari, in his ' Life of Girolamo da Carpi,' mentions having seen ' a very beautiful book of antiquities, drawn and measured by the hand of Bramantino,' and to have noticed among those designs ' the church of San Pietro in Ciel d'Oro at Pavia.'

PLATES 3 & 4.

ABBEY OF CHIARAVALLE, NEAR MILAN.

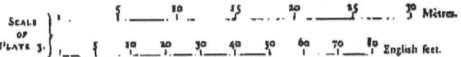

IN the year of grace 1135, on the 22nd of January, this monastery was founded in honour of the visit to Milan, in the previous year, of Saint Bernard, abbot of Clairvaux. In 1221 this church was consecrated by Don Enrico, archbishop of Milan, on the 2nd of May, and dedicated to S. Mary of Chiaravalle. An inscription to this effect in Latin, placed between the church and cloister, fixes the date of the foundation of both the monastery and church of Chiaravalle.

They stand amidst fat pastures and fertile fields, rendered such by the Cistercian monks, who ranked amongst the first to reclaim the Milanese marshlands by drainage. Of old this territory was called Rovegnano: subsequently it was named after S. Bernard's Monastery of Clairvaux, in Champagne, where his new order of friars had their first establishment. This Italian abbey by little and little became greatly enriched, both by means of numerous legacies from noble Milanese families and through the agricultural skill of the monks; so that, in the thirteenth century, the community owned above 64,000 perches of land. The arms of the order were a stork holding in its beak a crosier and a mitre between its feet. In this renowned abbey Archbishop Ottone Visconti lived longwhile and died. Here the flower of the Milanese nobility welcomed Beatrice d'Este as the bride of Galeazzo Visconti, and Cassone Torriani was made archbishop. The monastery was suppressed in 1798.

An irregular enclosure shuts in the abbey and the remains of the convent. The church is of Gothic architecture; the façade was in great part destroyed in the seventeenth century. The summit of its octagonal cupola commands an extensive and beautiful view. The church is spacious and grand, and some of its walls are covered with frescoes defaced by time. The choir is superb with its marvellous carvings. To the right is a great staircase, at the summit of which is a fresco by Bernardino Luini. Behind the choir, to the left, is a small rectangular cemetery, girt by a low wall; and round about stand little mortuary cells in the Gothic style, in each of which stood the monument of some distinguished family, as appears from the portraits, coats of arms and mottoes painted or sculptured there. Few of these cells now remain, and even these ill-preserved and ill-restored. Amongst such relics are still found certain gravestones of the Torriani; particularly those of Pagano and Martino della Torre, captains of the Milanese people in the thirteenth century. There is also a painting representing Manfredo Archinti before the Blessed Virgin, and the notorious heretic Wilhelmina (d. 1282).

Wherever the Carthusians founded a monastery of their order, their rule was to give to the church which had to be built the very same arrangements and character as belonged to the first church they raised. There were rules for the elevation of the cupola which served also as campanile, for the opening of the windows, for the direction to be followed from east to west, for the spot to be occupied by each altar; and many more into which we need not here enter. In the ancient duchy of Milan are several of these Carthusian convents, and their contiguous churches all resemble one another in style. Yet the Certosa of Chiaravalle exceeds the others in grandeur: the cupola-campanile, which in the sister churches is of very simple construction, in this is most elegant and ingenious. The solidity of its structure is admirable; it rests on four pointed arches only, which at a certain height support the cupola with its tower or campanile.

As seen in our Plate (3), the decoration of this campanile is architectural rather than ornamental, such decoration consisting merely of the small cornice arches. The means adopted for sustaining the lofty centre of the campanile are ingenious and worthy of remark: parallel with the sides of the actual campanile, two walls were raised at a certain distance and of divers altitudes, to form a sort of scarp or abutment of central support to the campanile; and thus, whilst solidity was secured, a graceful outline was produced, slim and pyramidal, in two divisions with steps; and as a great part of these little arches is so pierced that the sky shows through them, much beauty and elegance are added to the campanile. This edifice, or rather this spire, has several times been restored; not altogether, but as regards decorations, cornices, parapets, &c., because frost and heat frequently displace the bricks. When last restored it was bound with iron girders to avert possible future ruin. Through a like precaution, about the year 1500, the four ancient arches of the church were reinforced by a flying buttress to strengthen the piers.

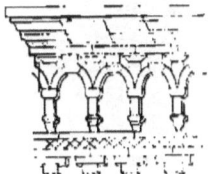 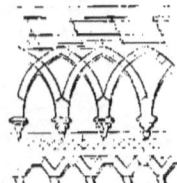

Details of Cornices, Arcades, Arches, etc., in the Abbey of Chiaravalle.

This church, both within and without, displays great simplicity of structure. The columns and arches of the interior are of terra-cotta bricks, now whitewashed, the bases and capitals only excepted.

Anyone viewing this and similar churches must feel that their style, which has been named Lombardo-Byzantine, is admirably suited to sacred edifices characterized as it is by grand simplicity, sufficiency of decoration, and solidity; all these seeming to express the primitive simplicity of Christianity in those first ages from which we have so far diverged. The interior has been ruined and defaced by whitewash: some of the 'barocco' chapels are, however, very pretty, and have on their walls and ceilings fine paintings, by good masters, of the seventeenth century. The cupola is painted in compartments and skilfully adorned with pleasing colours, in the taste and style of the fourteenth century.

G. L. Calvi,[1] towards the beginning of his life of Francesco Pecorori, architect, alluding to the impulse given to architecture about the end of

Details of Cornices, Arcades, Arches, etc., in the Abbey of Chiaravalle.

the thirteenth century by the Torriani and Matteo Visconti, thinks it not unlikely that this architect—the same who built the tower of San Gottardo at Milan—may also have designed the campanile of the abbey of Chiaravalle.

[1] Notizie sulla Vita e sulle Opere dei principali Architetti, Scultori e Pittori che fiorirono in Milano durante il governo dei Visconti e degli Sforza, ecc. ecc., raccolte ed esposte da Girolamo Luigi Calvi. Milano, 1859 e 1866.

The façade of the church was altered after 1600, when the not ungainly portico was constructed, which still remains. If it were wished to carry out the primitive design, so as to convey some idea of what the building must have been in its first completeness, one might substitute for the actual façade that of the church of Morimondo, where the Carthusians installed themselves almost simultaneously with their brethren of Chiaravalle.

O.

Middle portion of the Campanile of St. Gottardo at Milan.

Upper portion of the Campanile of St. Gottardo

THE CHURCH AND CAMPANILE OF SAN GOTTARDO, IN MILAN.

N the ruins of the church of San Giovanni al Fonte, a very ancient baptistery for males according to the rite of the Milanese church, Azzo Visconti, lord of Milan, erected the church of San Gottardo, adjacent to the royal palace. Of this church there now remain only the terra-cotta apse behind the choir, and the very fine campanile. (See Plates 5, 6.)

The chronicler Fiamma, who lived soon after Azzo, thus describes it: ' This magnificent chapel is enclosed by lofty walls, and roofed by three vaults ; and possesses admirable pictures in gold and azure,[1] of a marvellous workmanship. In the principal chapel, where stands the high altar, are screens made of metals and gems. There are portrayed sundry incidents of the life of the Madonna ; and there are some wonderful windows ; nor do all the kingdoms of the world contain a more wonderful work. The choir is wainscoted with finely-wrought ivory, and contains two pulpits, great and high, also of ivory ; a sight stupendous to behold. Many altars are there ornamented with gold and silk, and other things, such as cannot be fully recounted or described.'

This same Fiamma thus writes of the campanile of San Gottardo: ' At one side of the church is built the campanile of terra-cotta, adorned from summit to base with small marble columns, which give great delight to the gazer.'

On this tower was placed the first clock which struck the hours in Milan, and the contiguous Via delle Ore derived from it the name which it still bears.[2]

[1] It is presumable that these pictures were by Giotto ; in fact, Vasari writes that, in 1333, Giotto was already painting in Milan.

[2] The first mechanical clock was erected in Padua ; an opinion held also by Moinet (Nouveau Traité Général d'Horlogerie) and by Dubois (Histoire de l'Horlogerie) ; though they agree in assigning priority of date to the clock invented in 1324 by the English Benedictine Wallingford.

Both the church and the tower of San Gottardo represent to us fairly how architecture flourished in those days, especially in Upper Italy.

Hope, in his 'Historical Essay on Architecture,' describes this tower as

Details of Tower of San Gottardo.

'entirely woven over with small columns, some supported by its body, others projecting on brackets, all crowned by round-headed arches.' But whoever studies this building attentively finds much more than this; besides various lessons in the æsthetics of the art, he derives from it valuable practical hints as to the suitable employment of terra-cotta.

During five centuries this tower has braved the inclemency of the seasons without incurring noticeable traces of decay, although it has not been repaired for so long a time that weeds grew freely upon it, which, insinuating between the chinks their thread-like roots and suckers, by little and little do serious damage to buildings. And beyond this it must be remembered that Lombardy, and especially Milan, surrounded as it is by an involved network of canals and by immense meadow-lands artificially irrigated at all seasons, is subject in late autumn and in winter to dense and persistent fogs. In spite of these, terra-cotta ornaments, even such as are elaborately wrought and projecting with delicate workmanship, have not been at all injured in consequence. The

Details of Tower of San Gottardo.   *Tiles of Conical Roof, San Gottardo.*

architect, mistrusting perhaps the resisting power of terra-cotta against stress of wind, snowfall, fogs, hail, prolonged spring rains, fiery dog-days of summer, took care to furnish the tower windows with stone coigns; a vain precaution, since careful inspection of these windows reveals that the stone rather than the terra-cotta has suffered, however slightly, from the assaults of time.

This admirable solidity is owing to excellence of material and to scrupulous care in adjusting the bricks. Several writers have noticed the skill with which, in those days, bricks were arranged and fixed; the cement used for binding them together was of quicklime mixed with very fine sand taken from the river bed. This lime was dissolved in plenty of water, so as to flow in a thin liquid upon the various strata of bricks, forming itself so slight a stratum that the seam between the bricks is now barely discernible.

These bricks, as has been noticed by the brothers Sacchi,[1] were of varying form and structure, according to the different parts of the edifice in which they were placed. In rectilineal parts the dimensions of each brick were about one foot in length, three inches in depth, and six in breadth. When circular walls were in question, each brick presented a proportional part of an arch,

San Gottardo.

Arcade on Fourth Story of San Gottardo.
Pillars resting on projecting Brackets

more or less curved according to the expansion of the wall's circle. If those long string-courses, which from base to roof decorated the outside of the apses, were composed of bricks or of sandstone, these were then shaped to three-quarters of a circle. As to the order of their position in walls, the usual method was adhered to, of placing the centre of one brick above the junction of the two immediately below it.

[1] Antichità romantiche d' Italia. Milano, 1828

The name of the architect of the church and campanile of San Gottardo and of other fine buildings erected by order of Azzo Visconti, remained long unknown. In our own day, Signor G. L. Calvi, a learned and diligent writer on mediæval art,[1] has succeeded in discovering 'a slab anciently inserted in the wall towards the base of the tower;' a slab on which, 'although coated by repeated whitewashings,' he was able to decipher, 'Magister Franciscus de Pecoraris de Cremonâ fecit hoc opus.'

It is to be deplored that the contiguous royal palace, by a barbarous decree of the Spanish governor Ponze de Leon, has been defaced by a certain Ambrogio Pessina, who substituted for the fine Lombardic style a clumsy nondescript, destroying the noble windows of terra-cotta. This palace was finally modernised by order of the Austrian Archduke Ferdinand, after designs by Piermarini.

The magnificent sepulchral monument which enclosed the remains of Azzo Visconti, was broken to pieces at the rebuilding of the church of San Gottardo, but the fragments were preserved in Milan by the noble family of Trivulzi.   O.

[1] Notizie sulla Vita e sulle Opere dei principali Scultori e Pittori che fiorirono in Milano durante il governo dei Visconti e degli Sforza, raccolte ed esposte da G. L. Calvi. Milano, 1859.

Campanile of the Church of the Carmine

PLATES 7, 8, 9, 10 & 11.

THE CHURCH OF SANTA MARIA DEL CARMINE, PAVIA.

Scale
OF
Plate 7.

ALL writers who have treated of this church agree as to the excellent materials used in building it. Amongst them Malaspina of Sannazaro, in his Guide to Pavia,[1] speaks thus : 'The church of the Carmine is a vast edifice, erected in 1373; and although belonging to the then dominant style commonly termed Gothic, as is proved by its long narrow aisles and pointed arches, yet as it is exempt from insignificant and obtrusive details, and is graced with grand and harmonious proportions, the result is a majestic and impressive church ; and this, through the excellence of its material, which is indeed terra-cotta, but being smooth and joined with a very small portion of first-rate lime, endures almost as if it were formed of hewn stone.'

Thus we have a fresh proof that, sound rules being observed, brick wears better than certain qualities of stone. In the structure of this church the sculptures jut out very noticeably, and are carefully wrought with such surface inequalities as impart salience to those points which should catch the eye and produce effect. The number of figures surrounding the great rose-window in the centre of the façade (see Plate 9), as also of those surrounding the windows and door-jambs, is great : their arrangement is complicated ; and they are composed of countless bricks ; yet so neatly joined and polished are the figures, and so gracefully rounded, as to appear each of a single block.

[1] Pavia, 1819.

The same admirable perfection of work is found in other monuments of those times; which renders it probable that the masons, after placing the bricks one by one, must have mounted up to them to give the last polish and finishing touches. On no other supposition can we explain the high finish of their workmanship; nor can we in any case understand why they preferred thus putting together so many small pieces, instead of, according to modern practice, availing themselves of larger blocks.

The remains of the church of the Carmine, the sides and the campanile

Side Window in West Front of St. M. del Carmine, Pavia.

(see annexed Plates 7 to 11), form a grand and colossal whole. Compared with the façade, the sides appear little decorated; thick walls and strong piers and abutments sustain the thrust of the internal arcades, the whole being constructed of an enormous quantity of bricks: the cornices are few; here and there appears a niche, or an isolated coat of arms. Yet this imposing mass, with its ancient dusky-red tint, fails not to produce the effect of grandeur, severity, and mystery, proper to a place of worship: thus the architecture accords with the material, and the material with the architecture.

Nor must such marked simplicity of structure be attributed to mean economy or paucity of ideas: it seems to have been designed purely with a view to effect; for close examination of the edifice reveals that, in its construction, endless repetitions were eschewed, whilst, on due occasion, variety was aimed at. Thus we recognise a variety of figures in the small capitals, and especially in the little brackets which support the small cornice-arches; whilst, from time to time, the cornices themselves are interrupted with the sole object of breaking the monotony of continuity.

This style of architecture is effective, whether a view of the edifice be commanded from an extensive open place; or whether, as is the case with this church, its sides or back be blocked up amongst houses or narrow streets. If looked at from below upwards, and close at hand, the perspective lines diverge and vary, whilst the piers and walls assume gigantic proportions.

The majority of ancient churches were, at a later period, whitewashed or rebuilt; so that it is exceptional to find one which, like this of the Carmine at Pavia, retains its original inner structure of uncoated brick. This structure is very simple, consisting of three aisles; massive columns, of about ninety centimètres in diameter, support semicircular arches, the whole composed of bricks of that dark-red tint to which allusion has already been made, a tint characteristic of highly-baked brick; and as the windows of this church are high and few, a dim and evanescent light imparts to the interior an aspect of mysterious gloom, apt to foster abstraction and meditation. Nothing distracts the eye; the whole effect culminates in the high altar raised some considerable height.

The construction of the columns and round piers, all alike of brick, deserves careful study, evincing as it does consummate art; for, notwithstanding their thousands of component pieces, their shape appears faultlessly cylindrical. Each brick is somewhat bulky, being nine centimètres thick (high) and seventy long; and so neatly are they fitted and joined together, that it is only on very close inspection that the joints become distinguishable, and not even so much as the point of a penknife can be inserted between brick and brick. Yet, to study these piers and columns thoroughly, one must needs dismember them, at least partially, piece from piece.

I

We have said, and we repeat it—the artists of those times knew how to stamp on each building its special and distinctive character. In general, therefore, they were not prone to using in their decorations coloured fillets, or marble, or any other ornament producing harsh contrast, or likely to break the tone or design of the decoration: thus they preserved to sacred architecture its grave, solemn, and religious character. It was in houses, palaces, secular buildings, that they gave loose to fancy, lavishing on these paintings, coloured fillets, marbles, &c. &c., to divert the eye by an agreeable variety.

The tower or campanile of the Carmine at Pavia (Plate 11) exemplifies this principle, being treated as a structure independent of the church, and rearing its comely head above the city. Being designed to be seen from afar, greater variety and brilliancy have been bestowed upon it, and this effect is produced by boldly contrasted colours and fillets.

To promote the erection of this church, from its very commencement the produce of a tax levied on widowers contracting a second marriage was assigned to it. The payment of this tax protected them from the importunity of the youths who used to beset them with demands for money to be lavished on feasts and merry-makings.

O.

Part of the Church of St Francesco at Pavia

PLATE 12.

THE CHURCH OF SAN FRANCESCO, IN PAVIA.

A PORTION OF THE FAÇADE.

HAVE had to represent this building by a geometrical elevation show-
ing the façade, in order to convey its just proportions and divisions;
but, for the lovers of picturesque perspective, a far more advantageous
view is obtained laterally, and I should say that this is the pictorial effect aimed
at by the architect who designed it. The architects of those days appear, before
commencing a work, to have foreseen its pictorial or perspective effect; and this
church, situated at the opening of long roads, presents a picturesque aspect from
every point of approach, and assumes an air of importance beyond what really
belongs to it. I would gladly have portrayed it for the sake merely of its fine
effect; but have abandoned this intention in order to show, with how little cost,
and with what great economy, a façade may be completely decorated. The main
secret consists in conceiving a good composition, combining unity of idea with
variety of line, otherwise ornamentation the most ingenious, choice, and elaborate,
would fail of its effect, and be but labour lost: a risk sadly exemplified in modern Milan, whose architects load ornament on ornament with much pedantry
and hair-splitting, observing every rule of finish and precision; in spite of which
their works lack effect, and fail even to command notice from passers-by. The
old men, on the other hand, ignored a hundred pedantries, and achieved what was
pictorially and scenically effective. They have indeed left us monuments of signal
painstaking and exactness; yet often precision, perfect symmetry, and equality
of treatment were neglected; whilst, thoroughly understanding the nature of their
materials, they took heed to obtain these of sound quality; and thus their structures have withstood the ravages of time, as is the case with this church of San

Francesco, which, in spite of no special care having been bestowed on its forms, and on the juncture of its bricks, yet as a whole is well preserved. And be it noted, in proof of the suitability and economy of terra-cotta decorations, that rich and complete as those of San Francesco appear, yet the dominant forms, as of the figures, squares, rhombs, and balls, are always the same, sometimes studding the cornices in straight lines, and sometimes following the curve of the arches. This façade, at any rate, required to be faced with the usual smooth oblong bricks, and those employed differ from the common type only by change of shape; whence it is presumable that the expense incurred for material exceeded by but little the cost of ordinary bricks, and was thus augmented only by the shaping-process, and the longer time it took the work-man to fix each piece in its place; a work in which, be it remembered, scrupulous precision was not observed.

L.

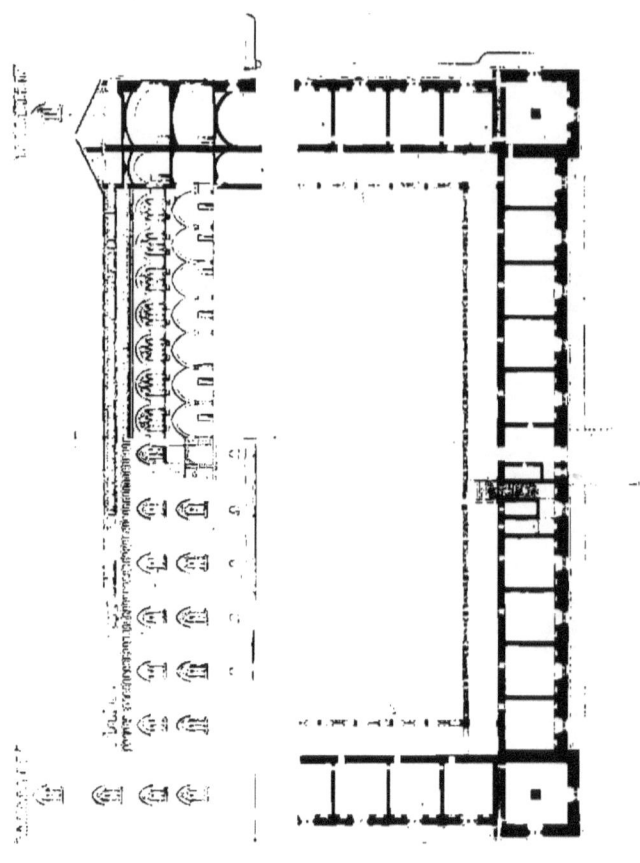

Bridge from the south of the Piazza, say A.

PLATES 13, 14 & 15.

THE CASTLE OF PAVIA.

SCALE }
OF }
PLATE 13. } 10 20 30 40 50 60 70 80 90 100 English feet.

10 20 30 40 50 60 Mètres.

THE ancient historian Breventano thus describes the Castle of Pavia erected by Galeazzo Visconti :—

'The castle or palace was one of the finest buildings to be seen in those times, if the fury of the French[1] had not defaced its finest portion towards the park by their artillery. This range of building was of capacity sufficient to lodge the court of any king or emperor whatsoever. It is of square form, and has in the midst a large courtyard commodious for the holding of jousts, tournaments, and other princely games, surrounded by arcades both above and below, with marble columns, and with staircases constructed in such a manner that a horseman could mount to the summit. The halls and other chambers, both the upper and the lower ones, are all vaulted, and almost all painted with various comely histories and devices, while the ceilings were coloured with finest azure, in which divers animals of gold, as lions, leopards, tigers, greyhounds, setters, &c. appear to roam to and fro. On the side destroyed by the French artillery on the 4th September, 1527, was a vast saloon, 120 feet long by 40 wide, all decorated with admirable figure subjects, representing hunting or fishing parties and jousts with various other pastimes of the dukes and duchesses of this state. In the middle of this large apartment was a great

---

[1] He alludes to the then recent damage done to Pavia in 1527 by the French, under the command of Lautrec.

K

window, 20 feet wide by 24 high, with a balcony which jutted out a distance
of 12 feet over the moat, where, on summer evenings, the tables were con-
veniently laid, and enjoying the fresh breeze, the inmates took their repast to
the sound of gay instruments. Beneath this fine edifice all the way round are
double cellars: one part receiving light through windows overlooking the moat
which is very wide and full of water, and the other part receiving it through
windows facing towards the inner court. In these cellars were also the stables
and many handmills.

'This palace had four great towers, but now there remain only two
towards the city; the other two were broken down by the artillery of Gascon
Lautrec . . . .'

Breventano, after speaking of a wonderful clock placed to the right hand of
the castle, and of the famous library containing the precious collection of MSS.
formed by Petrarch, the catalogue of which is found in the Milanese Library of
the Brera, goes on to mention the pavements, 'lozenged in divers colours as if
they were glazed.' He specifies one room, which ' was in the third tower, and
was called the apartment of the mirrors, because the whole of its vaulted ceiling
was covered with glass squares as large as the palm of a hand, all of varied
colours, like those which are seen in churches, figured after the similitude of
men, beasts, plants, and flowers, wrought of gold ; and which, when smitten
by the sun's rays, gave back such clearness and splendour as dazzled the sight.
The floor of this beautiful room was all of Mosaic, and around it were great
stalls for sitting, all inlaid at the back as high as a man's hand would reach.' . . .

Of this magnificent dwelling, now degraded to a barrack, there remain no
more than two great towers and some fragments of the arcades. It would seem
that this castle was from time to time enlarged and embellished. The above-
quoted Breventano speaks in fact of one large saloon erected by a duke of
Milan ; a saloon, 120 feet long by 24 wide, constructed ' for matches at pal-
lone (ball) and other games in the rainy season.' . . . Amongst the artists
summoned to adorn this castle, Calvi[1] names the sculptor and architect,
Bernardino of Venice.

---

[1] Calvi, *op cit.*

The three façades of the quadrangle with arcades are differently decorated; they present, that is, on one side, windows of one style, on another side of another, and on the third of a third. They are ascribed to the fourteenth century, and are a medley of Gothic and Bramantesque. These arcades and windows are very grand. In the illustrations which we give of them (Plates 14, 15) we perceive how large a proportion of the ornament is constructed of terra-cotta; only the columns, the capitals, and a few cornices are of stone; the fillets and the imitation marbles are, after the fashion of those times, painted in fresco with very bright colours, to counteract the excessive preponderance and uniformity of tint in the terra-cotta. In those days certain very beautiful colours, of which the secret is lost to us, were employed in fresco painting; amongst them yellow and green, as shown in the annexed illustrations. These colours produce a good effect; but it must not be supposed that all such things were executed with extraordinary care and precision; they were, on the contrary, coarsely treated, as, for instance, human figures, animals, flowers, &c. All was calculated for the coup d'œil, for optical and (so to speak) theatrical effect: here and there a point shows carelessness, with but slight connection and finish of workmanship. This last, indeed, was not required, for as the windows and decorations were high above the spectator, greater finish would have been labour thrown away.

It is noticeable that there remain many highly finished monuments in terra-cotta, dating from 1200 to 1500, and of these several are treated pictorially and with striking scenic effect. Terra-cotta may advantageously be employed in lieu of stone both for cheapness, and because the art of modelling gives the artist scope to work with greater freedom, and to reproduce the ideas dictated by fancy, just as the painter does with his brush. The public for the most part is satisfied with the general effect, and goes no further towards weighing whether all is finished and precise, but rather enjoys a sketch vigorous, harmonious, and of decided effect. The decorations of the Castle of Pavia are almost all in a state of dilapidation; scarcely a window can be found of which the ornaments remain complete: the colouring, indeed, is no longer recognisable by a common eye. The artist who produced the annexed plates of the Castle of Pavia, underwent such eye-training in the study of similar objects, patiently retracing every

mark, every shade, every hint of colour, every scratch, that he oftentimes succeeded in recovering what formerly existed.   From their present dilapidated condition we can form but a faint idea of the beauty of such edifices when newly
erected.   We now behold them partially in ruins, shorn of cornices, their
windows blocked-up, and paintings effaced or removed, and marred by subse-
quent blundering additions to the first design ; in a word, deficient in parts, or
with parts incongruous with the original plan.   To this must be added accu-
mulation of dirt, ornaments hidden here and there by mud, extensive oxidation, and the consequent blackening effect of the atmosphere, all together veil-
ing the general aspect of ancient edifices with a dusky grey tint.   With the
object, therefore, of more faithfully representing those monuments, which this
work aims at illustrating, the artist has in a measure recreated them, restoring
them partially, though only so far as their original aspect can be inferred from
what remains ; whilst, jealous for the truth, he seeks to preserve to whatever
monument he depicts, a certain antique tone, in order to prevent it from appearing an altogether new building.

                                                                    O.

Facade of the Cathedral of Crema

Window from the Front of the Cathedral — Genoa

Details of facade of the Cathedra

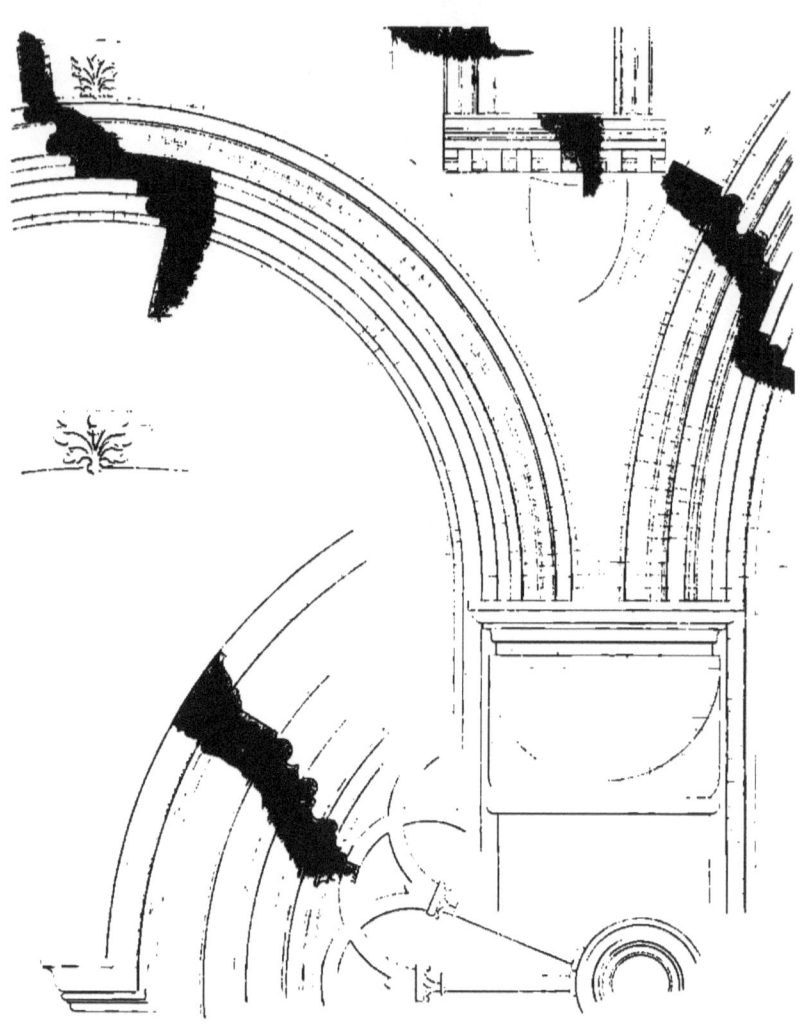

Details of façade of the Cathedral._ Crema.

PLATES 16 TO 22.

FAÇADE WINDOWS AND OTHER DETAILS OF THE CATHEDRAL OF CREMA.

An altogether remarkable structure : chiefly for the unusual colour of its terra-cotta; in fact, I have as yet seen no second specimen of this shade of light orange colour shown in the Plate, representing a part of the spire (*vide* Plate 24), which produces a good effect, and which, on the southern exposure, subjected to the sun's blaze and frequent rain-washings, assumes even a brilliant surface. The fine material (terra-cotta) remains to the present day in excellent preservation, and the angles are as sharp as if newly cut. It is true, indeed, that many individual bricks appear reddish, blackish, or grey; and perhaps it was not possible for the clay to be cleared from every trace of oxide of iron or other mineral.

The arrangement, as seen in the annexed Plate (16), is of extreme simplicity, yet very richly decorated. The form of the main arches and the lesser upper arches rising and falling on their small supporting columns, evince the influence

---

* There is a church at Lodi Vecchio, built of bricks of a yellow ochreous shade. The ordinary red tint can be avoided by rejecting clays impregnated with metallic oxides; and not only white but a variety of colours are attainable by due management. The hardest brick when struck will emit sparks like a flint.

L

of still-powerful Byzantine tradition ; whilst the foliage, small pointed arches, and other details give to the building a character such as became fully developed at a later date. Whence I deduce that this church was constructed either towards the end of the thirteenth or possibly at the very beginning of the fourteenth century. I have failed to identify the architect, but his name matters little : this unknown architect has left an enduring monument of his technical science and artistic taste. Of all the edifices I know, this displays the best and most careful workmanship. Close inspection is necessary to discover how much precision, skill, and finish have been bestowed on those figures and that foliage, which to this day remain as if newly wrought. The patterns, composed of hundreds of pieces, present a surface as polished and unbroken as if cast in bronze ; the desired effect being achieved by the usual means of obtaining relief, exaggeration of hollows and of salient points ; as exemplified also in the church of the Carmine. The outline of the windows, which looks very squat, has that effect because of the introduction of numerous patterns in the jambs ; yet this imperfection is modified by adding to each window two small arches supported by very slight columns and producing a slim whole : thus these slim and elongated forms balance the squatness, and one portion supplies the just complement of the other. Observe how the upper windows (Plates 18, 19) have been cunningly, or rather cleverly, made less squat ; and why ? because the court fronting the façade is but 32 feet 6 in. in extent, and affords at best a distorting view-point, whence squatness would have appeared yet more squat ; a danger which the architect has met by greater lightness of the upper portion.

The variations introduced into the different windows (Plates 17, 18, 19, 20) afford an additional proof that the architects of those times were endowed with subtle artistic sense, and were in fact painters and poets in another medium : for their edifices and decorations are the obvious channels of their fancy ; repetition fatigued them ; and they endeavoured, on all occasions, to vary shapes and ornaments ; their ideas were mainly their own, for they lacked the multitudinous specimens and examples which have accumulated for us. Thus the meanness of our achievements illustrates how potent beyond all else are true talent and genuine vocation.

It would be interesting to examine both by what means the bricks have been united to form figures, &c., and also how they were wrought, &c.; but such investigations cannot be carried out, as they would entail the dismemberment of a piece for the sake of seeing into or under it. From my own observation of other buildings, I conclude that the methods used to secure, fix, and clench the bricks differ but slightly from those employed for inserting in walls fragments of stone or marble, as cornices, jambs, corbels, &c. &c.; the wall, that is, is built in zigzag, holes and recesses being left for the reception of each piece of terra-cotta, and hooks and iron nails added in case of need, there being this convenience attached to terra-cottas, that they can be hollowed out by hand. Only in using iron care must be taken thoroughly to imbed each piece of metal, as otherwise atmospheric action might cause rust and expansion to the detriment of the brickwork. Mortar should be applied in thin layers, as in thick masses it lacks tenacity. Plaster ('gesso') should be eschewed altogether, as no dependence can be placed on its durability. Thus terra-cottas possess two advantages: first, they can be easily fixed to the wall; and, secondly, each piece can be made lighter and diminished by the chisel.

I need not point out the elegance of the portal of this church. It is formed of white marble blackened by time, and is represented in our Plate 16.

L.

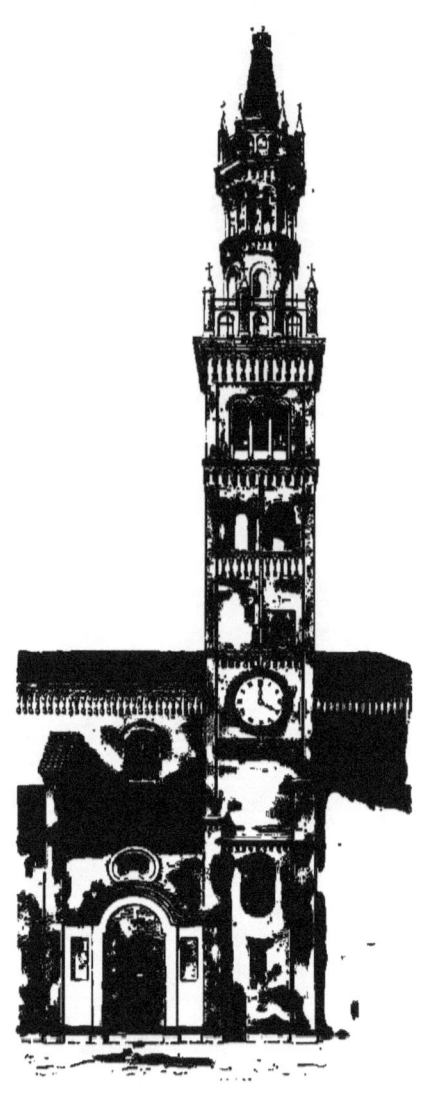

The „Campanile" of the Cathedral of Crema.

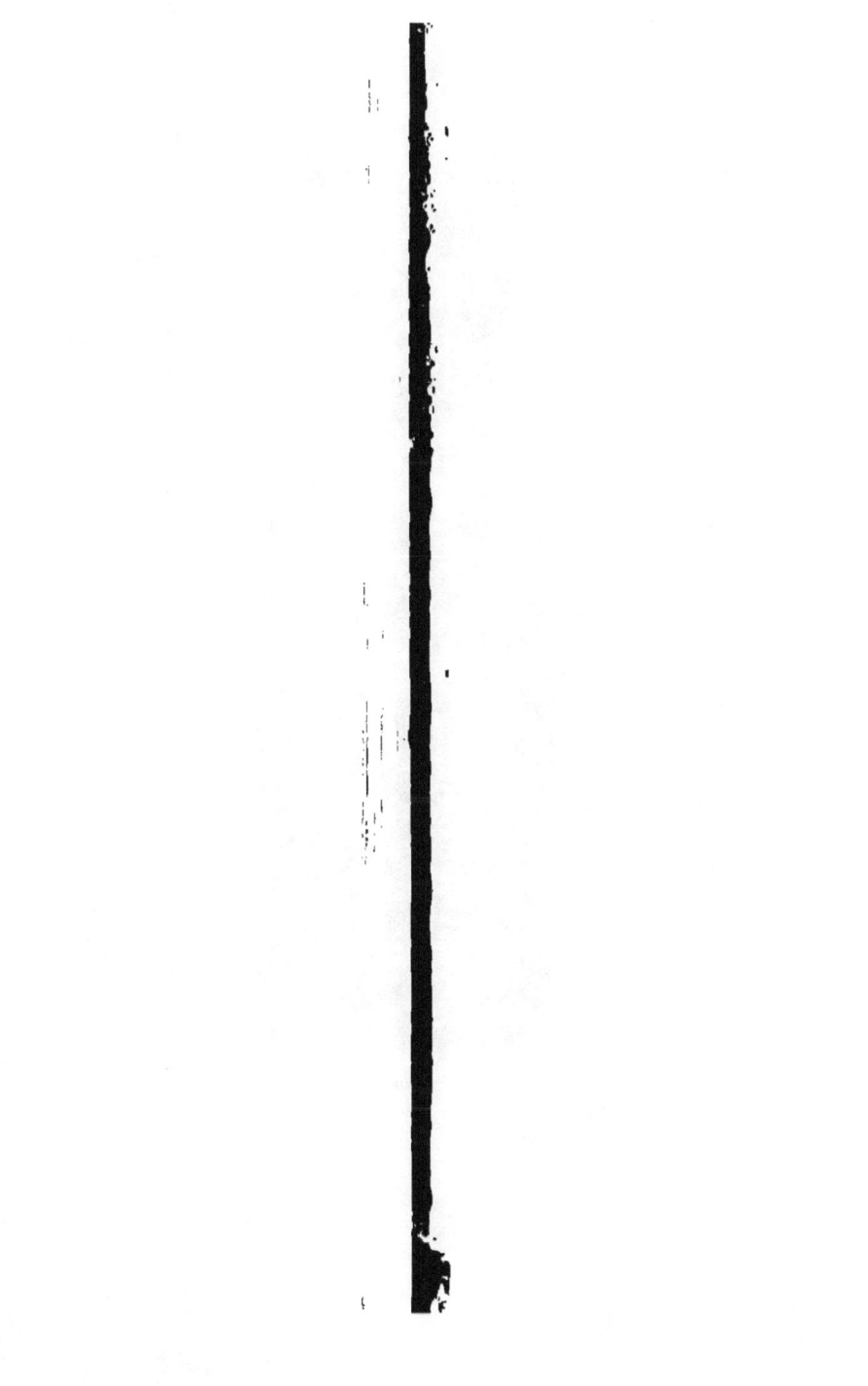

Part of the Campanile

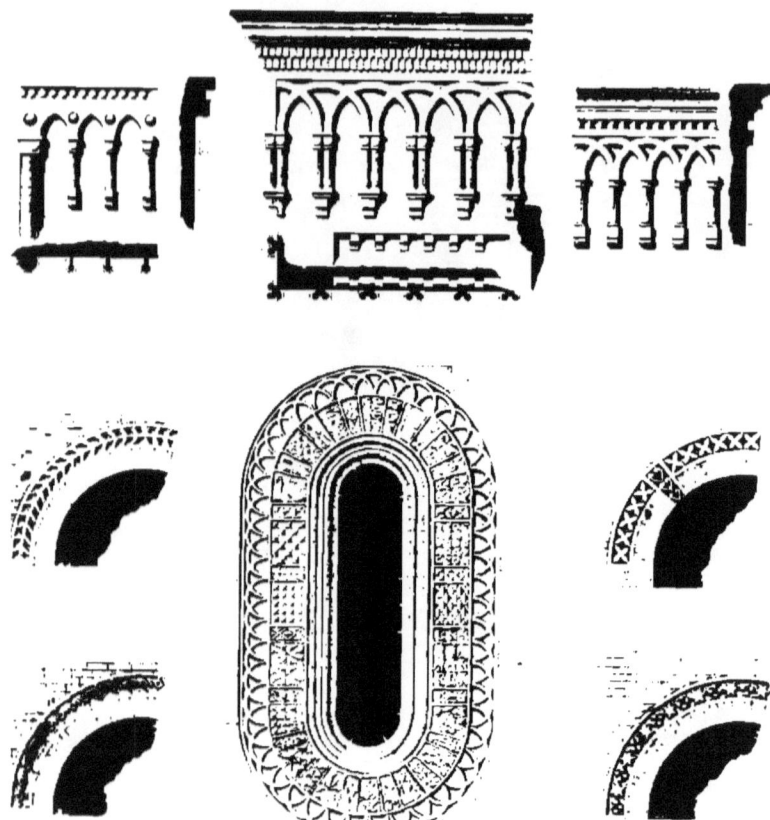

PLATES 23, 24 & 25.

CAMPANILE OF THE CATHEDRAL OF CREMA.

N the early days of the Middle Ages it was a special ambition of cities and communes to possess a fine campanile. The upper part of this campanile of Crema has evidently been elaborated with an eye to the utmost attainable elegance and beauty in that lofty portion which is visible from all points. It looks well with its openings even from a distance ; and, when such structures are well tapered, they cannot fail to produce a good effect ; most of all when light form, beautiful colour, and brilliant gilding are added. It is one proof of talent to know how to seize every means which art affords of achieving beauty. Although the free use of pointed arches might seem to indicate a change of style in the direction of the Gothic, I incline to believe that our architect had no intention of imitating this school : both church and campanile bear witness to a style already formed and established, which I name Lombard, because distinct alike from the Byzantine and from the Gothic.

Certain encircling ornaments, particularly those of the campanile windows, suggest an imitation of embroidery. (Plate 25.)

L.

Façade of the Church of St Rustico at Caravaggio.

PLATES 26 & 27.

FAÇADE OF THE CHURCH OF SS. FERMO E RUSTICO, AT CARAVAGGIO.

HAVE failed to discover who was the builder of this church. The style of its architecture is very elegant, and at the same time fully developed; and as it bears no trace of either Byzantine or Gothic influence, I call it Lombard, and assign it to the fourteenth century. The workmanship in marble of the well-designed entrance doorway, and the masterly execution of the terra-cottas, show an advanced stage of decorative art; whilst the carving of the statues, the arrangement more complicated than is observed in older buildings, the variety of line and of proportion bear witness to experience and mature taste. The perspective effect produced by sloping cornices and pinnacles, one rising above the other, is thoroughly picturesque and pleasing, as may be judged from our Plates. In my notes on the church of San Francesco, at Pavia, I have already insisted on the all-importance in building of judicious design, of just proportion, and, above all, of striking perspective. This church of San Rustico seen from afar is admirable for its very tapering lines; whilst a nearer leisurely inspection brings to light the high finish of its workmanship. The façade was evidently not commenced and completed by the same artist; much of the lower portion, the entrance-door excepted, appears to be by a different hand, as certain bricks are still visible in the wall apparently prepared for an arrangement of the windows which was never carried out.

A peculiar feature of frequent occurrence in the architecture of those times is a huge façade, towering in parts above the roofs of the aisles connected with it, and presenting, as it were, a vast screening frontage. The idea, doubtless,

was to impart an air of magnitude to the church, but such expedients should be
eschewed: a sounder rule is, that outside aspect and scale should correspond
with internal dimensions.

The upper part of the west front is tinged with a deeper shade of red than
the lower, the bricks having obviously been coloured red either with varnish
or with oil pigment. Be it which it may, it remains in good preservation, and
has resisted that oxidation which mostly dyes old brick of a dark grey hue.
The story goes, though I vouch not for its authenticity, that this colour was
prepared from the blood of oxen, which, sinking into the brick, stopped up the
pores with a kind of enamel that kept out damp and defied oxidation.

L.

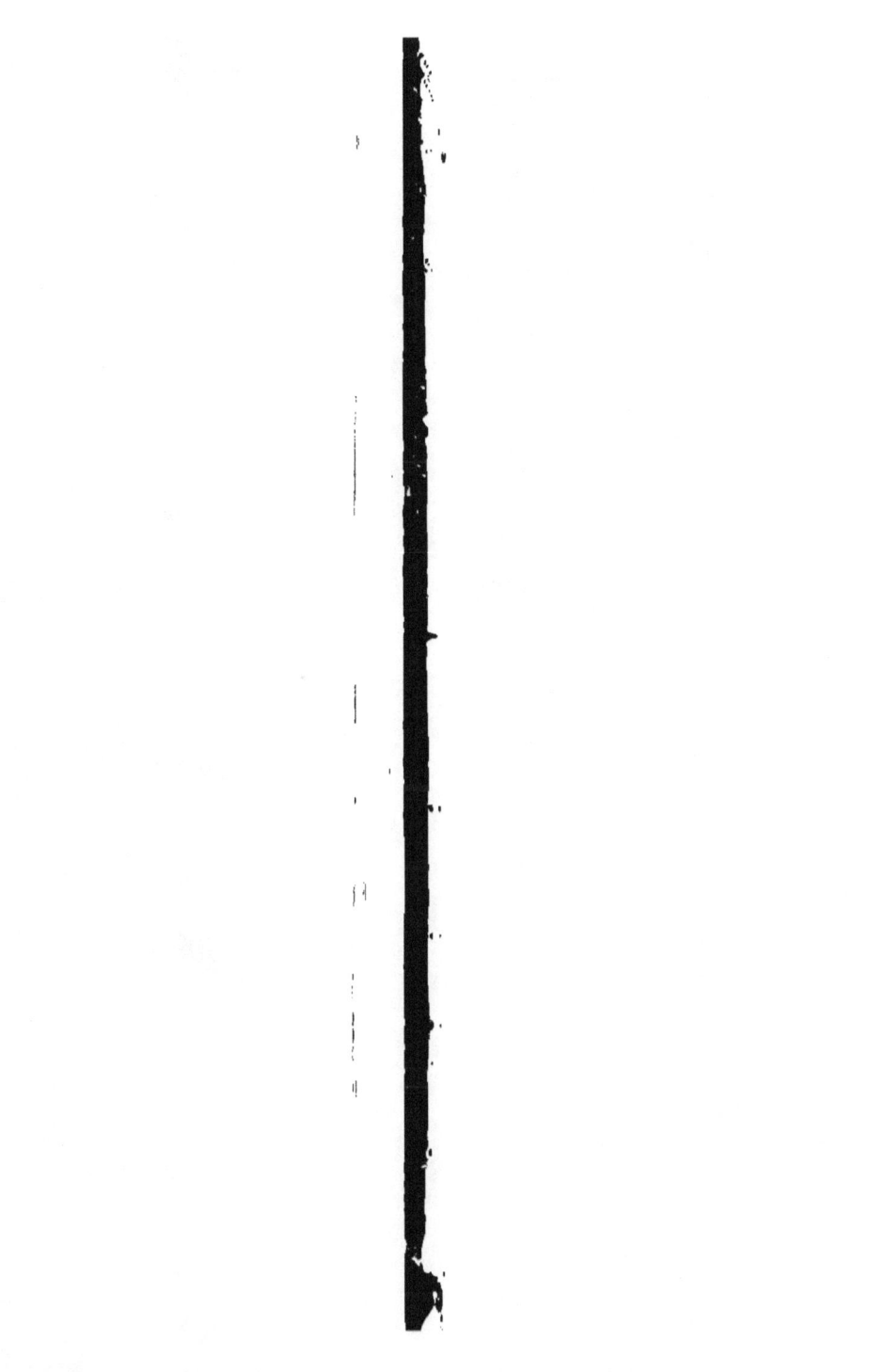

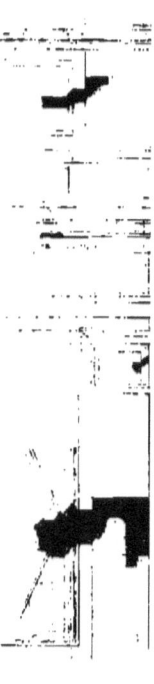

PLATE 28.

THE CAMPANILE OF SAN RUSTICO, CARAVAGGIO.

BEHIND the church of San Rustico stands a little church or shrine, like that in the Borgo di Caravaggio, and belonging to the same order of architecture, both having probably been designed by one and the same architect, perhaps Giovanni Battista Battagli of Lodi, who flourished about the end of the fourteenth century. Artists usually term the end of the fourteenth and beginning of the fifteenth centuries the epoch of the Renaissance even for architecture and its decorations; but I demur to this, recognising no season of revival but one unbroken course of progress. And if they would name Renaissance a return to the Greco-Roman type, I maintain that the classic school awes me by no authority beyond that of the equally reasonable Byzantine, Lombard, or Gothic. The Bramantesque, or Cinquecento style, being in fact the old Greco-Roman enriched by good ideas borrowed from other orders, seems to me well suited to modern Italy; it is at once beautiful and elegant, as exemplified in the façade of the Certosa of Pavia, and in many noble monuments of the period.

The architect who designed this campanile was one of those who, like Bramante, reverted to the classic style.

This campanile, although its summit was never completed, deserves the Plate we give of it as illustrating how such a structure may be adequately decorated by the economical use of simple brick. Had it been left plain it must

N

equally have been built of brick ; and the cost would then scarcely have been
less than was actually incurred to combine four square walls with varied cornices and sundry compartments, thus investing the entire campanile with an
architectural character.   To unite simplicity with thrift is a far more difficult
task than might be imagined, as architects know to their cost; and this
campanile is a fair specimen of such a combination.

L.

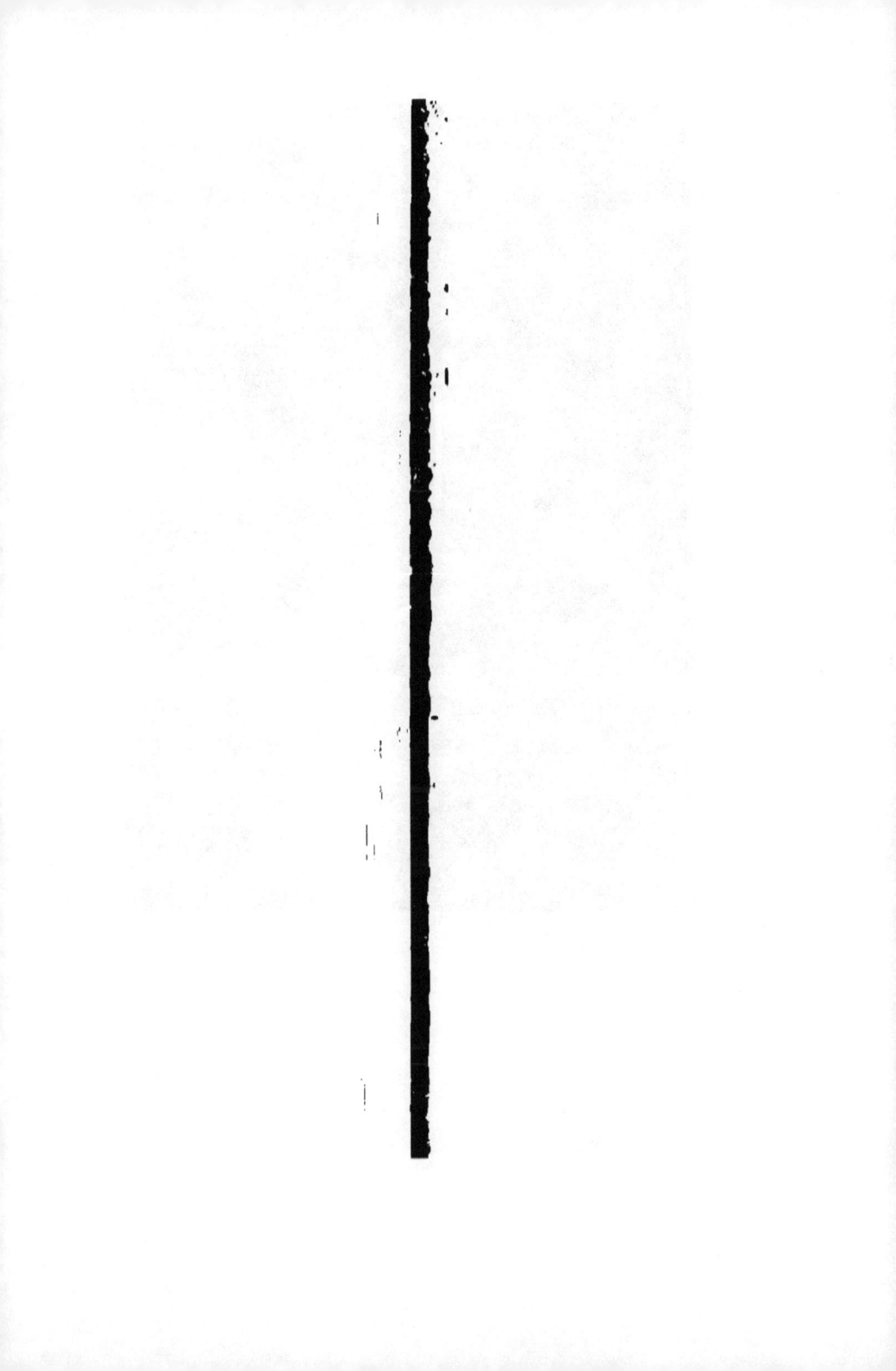

Various spires from the Certosa near Pavia.

PLATES 29 TO 33.

THE CERTOSA AND CONVENT OF PAVIA.

SCALE
OF
PLATE 32. 10 20 30 40 50   English feet

Mètre.

FIVE miles from Pavia, opposite the village of Torre del Mangano, on the 8th September, 1396, Galeazzo Visconti, duke of Milan and lord of Pavia, laid the first stone of the famous Certosa of Pavia. Three years later the convent was tenanted by twenty-six Carthusian monks, to whom the duke assigned as endowment various neighbouring farms, which produced a considerable income ; charging this, however, with a fixed annual sum devoted to carrying on the unfinished building.

It is not our purpose to give a description of this magnificent monument, which the historian Guicciardini calls ' perhaps the finest monastery beyond all others :' nor of the abundant art treasures which it contains : these have already been repeatedly described.[1] We will confine ourselves to those portions of the cloister which are embellished by terra-cottas.

We think we are correct in stating that the architects who took part in erecting the Certosa of Pavia belonged to that body of artists who professed modern freemasonry, and which considered the individual artistic intelligence of each member as the common stock of all. From this society proceeded technical knowledge, the fruit of long practice in the art of con-

---

[1] See also L. Gruner's text to his ' Fresco-Decorations ' (part ii. p. 49 ff.), where all that is worth knowing of the history of this magnificent convent is given.

* N 2

struction ; secrets of solidity in building ; rules for the preparation and the use of material ; mastery of the divers properties of stones, of clays, of lime, of plaster, of timber, &c. In fact, in the structures of those times, the ground-plan of the building, the arrangement of supporting piers, the skilfully masked buttresses helping to resist the thrust of the arch, the bulge of walls, convey valuable lessons. It is very exceptional for cornices or decorations formed of terra-cotta or of bricks, to be found even at this day broken or displaced by

General View of the Church of the Certosa, Pavia.

any degree of exposure to the elements, so that, as we have already observed in speaking of the tower of San Gottardo, this material has defied and still defies frost, damp, dog-days, and, in one word, all sorts of bad weather. The injuries sometimes suffered by such structures are traceable either to original inexactness in fitting piece to piece, or to violent shocks which they have undergone, or to the slow unceasing growth of weeds which, taking root in seams and chinks, exerted a wedge-like power. Generally speaking the mortar used to unite stones and bricks was so well mixed, and composed of such just proportions and of such fine and thoroughly purified sand, that time has but conferred upon it a hardness and solidity beyond those of the very bricks and stones.

In those times there existed neither appropriate academies, nor public schools of art, nor works gathered together for consultation; yet we find in those speci-

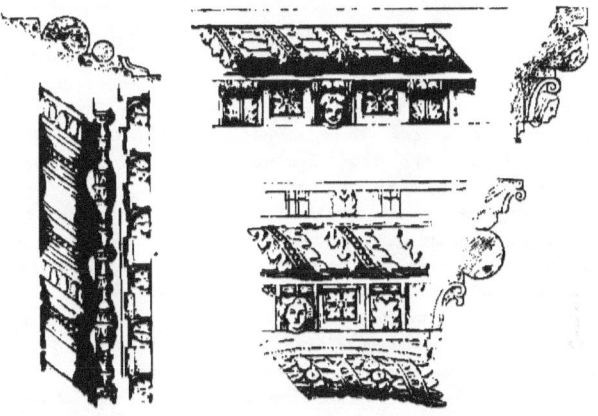

Terra-cotta Pilaster, Certosa.   *Cornices of Terra-cotta, Certosa.*

mens derived from the Certosa of Pavia all that may interest a student of the constructive art, an art always connected with the beautiful and with poetry. The Certosa of Pavia, both by the suppression of the Cistercian monks who inhabited it, and by the loss of the sheets of lead which protected its roof, has certainly sustained some, yet only slight, damage; neither have walls given way, nor fissures been formed. The artists of those days were all somewhat encyclopædic : architects were at once sculptors and painters, and thus had ample scope for the play of fancy. Before the first stone was laid they foresaw the pictorial and perspective effect of the finished building; an all-important perception, not perhaps sufficiently observed at the present day.

o

From whatever point the Certosa of Pavia is viewed, the perspective lines appear admirably disposed; either pointed, or pyramidal, or curved, or jutting, &c., they offer infinite varieties of perspective; all is harmonised, but with variations which relieve the eye and agreeably take possession of the fancy. Guided by a powerful instinct, those artists, besides variety of form and line, studied combination of materials and colours, relieving the too great darkness of terra-cotta by interpolation of marble and surfaces of stucco.

At San Lanfranco, a church in the outskirts of Pavia, part of the cortile and ancient cloister still remain; and we find there replicas in terra-cotta of some details in the cortile of the Certosa and in the church Del Carmine, of Pavia, several of these pieces bearing the inscription, *Abbas Lucas, F. F.* 1464 (Abbot Luke caused to be made); from which may be inferred that the terra-cottas of the period all originated in one workshop.

Studying the cortiles of the Certosa of Pavia, the cloisters which encircle them appear at the first glance uniform; but close examination reveals, on the two opposite sides, variety of composition or diversity of arrangement, and fresh combinations of geometric forms, of square with circular, all justly proportioned, sometimes large and sometimes small. So also we find, on running the eye along, the statuettes and small heads alternating with statues, busts, and heads on a large scale, and the inlaid work that surrounds them with foliage, little birds and fruit; the masses all most richly ornamented. Amid such pomp of fancy and abundance of invention, simplicity, which is ever coupled with true beauty, bears rule, and makes clear the primary conception and arrangement; whilst an examination of the minute details of foliage or small heads in terra-cotta brings to light the exquisiteness of the Gothic carving, grapes and other fruits appearing as of the most luscious kinds, thanks to skilful management of their little shadows. Everywhere is traceable the hand of the painter-poet, who having conceived the many-sided whole, wrought it out piece by piece, including each minor detail, whether of statuette or of small head, the whole being fashioned by a master-hand, and instinct with piety, energy, life.

It must, however, be allowed, that the artists who had to do with the Certosa of Pavia owed much to that civilisation which already, in matters of art, had made great progress, and had become widely diffused, and that in building this famous monastery they enjoyed a very appropriate field for displaying their talents; while the funds, the want of which so often strangles genius, were not lacking to them. Those who had charge of the growing work were Cistercian monks, men devoted to the contemplative life, and misanthropic rather in semblance than in reality; who, whilst ostensibly detached from worldly things, yet took pleasure in animating the walls, the doors, the passages, the pilasters, &c. of their cloister with artistic life.

The monastery is an extensive parallelogram of about 140 yards by 110, and is surrounded on its four sides by a lofty and ample cloister formed of 123 arches. Along each of three sides of the cloister 24 cells are ranged symmetrically.

The outer southern side, which looks towards the two unequally sized courts of the Certosa, the larger of these being of very considerable extent, presents the most splendid elevation. Below is seen a graceful portico, of which the arches are supported by slim, well-proportioned pillars, formed alternately of white marble and of Veronese mandorlato, and crowned by varied capitals, the arches themselves being corniced with terra-cottas of a fine fiery red colour: the roof too is visible, which formerly displayed a pleasing grey tint when coated with lead. Behind is seen one side of the church with its chief tapering steeple, which serves as cupola, and is all of white stone pierced and wrought into small arcades. Beyond the porticoes stretches a range of piers which serve to buttress the internal arches of the nave. These enclose a series of most elegant side-chapels built of white marble, in the best style of Cinquecento architecture, each different from its fellows, all enriched with little figures, grotesques, little cupolas, little pinnacles, and such like; the white marble relieved admirably by the dark background of bricks and terra-cotta cornices on the side of the central aisle or nave, the roof of which is supported by two ranges of arcaded galleries meant for passage, whilst the arches of these are sustained by pilasters. To enhance the beauty of this coup d'œil, the principal cornices facing towards the cortiles were coloured with a varnish resembling oil; the hues have now well nigh vanished, but enough remains to indicate how each part was coloured. Nay, the very chimneys which emerge from the convent roofs are designed with great architectural elegance; so prodigal were these men of artistic work, as though seeking in all directions a vent for their redundant imagination. Specimens of the chimneys and clock turret of the Certosa appear in the body of our work. (See Plate 33.)

· O.

Front view of Sta Maria in Strada at Monza

Principal entrance   Maria in Strada

PLATES 34 & 35.

SANTA MARIA IN STRADA, AT MONZA: THE FAÇADE AND
PRINCIPAL ENTRANCE.

SCALE
OF
PLATE 34.

HIS building, the work of Bonino di Campione, engineer and architect
of Milan Cathedral, belongs to the middle of the fourteenth century,
and to the dawn of a change in architectural style and ornamentation. The pupils or imitators of Giotto introduced into their decorations
geometrical figures, as squares, triangles, rhombs, rhomboids, hexagons, octagons,
circles, &c., which, in their hands, blended admirably with architectural lines
and ornaments; whilst, at the same time, the Gothic style came into fashion in
Italy. Hence arose and flourished in its day a mixed style compounded of
Lombard and Gothic, which combined geometrical forms with a little Gothic.
The designer of the Gothic cathedral of Milan would naturally be disposed to
produce another work of the same type, such as the church we are now
considering. At a period when the religious severity of elder times ceased to
be characteristic of the prevalent style of ecclesiastical building, it was very
readily abandoned in such a church, or rather shrine, as this of Santa Maria in
Strada. The upper part of this church is covered with terra-cotta ornaments:
the subjects of the squares, which form a sort of cornice and frame to the great
round window, and those which flank it on either side, are all different from one
another, and must, therefore, have been modelled one by one. This is also the
case with certain minor squares round the same window, with the door of

P

entrance, and with each leaf and ornament lavished on these arch-heads. In a word, every detail must have been wrought separately, and been treated as a theme on which the artist was left to the free exercise of his fancy within the resources of the plastic art.   The style of foliage is Gothic.   Below, towards the base, we find a region of colour commencing with gilded grounds; next come geometrical compartments, imitation marbles, and fillets of bright colours. The effect when new must have been magnificent.   Had the whole surface from top to bottom been covered with such patterns in terra-cotta, the result, though rich, would have wearied the eye by its monotony; but as it is, a wise arrangement of coloured details below throws out to advantage the upper portion.   No great precision was bestowed on each compartment and ornament; bricks are joined together in a somewhat slovenly fashion, straight lines and curves lack sweep and continuity, and the technical portions show negligence. Hence many of the terra-cottas have fallen out, and many are broken; the whole has suffered severely from frost and stress of weather; whilst of the doorway there now remains merely a fragment of the upper portion, and its general outline has only been guessed at by studying traces left on the wall by terra-cottas no longer there.   Neither was it a light matter to decipher the paintings, great patience being needed to elicit their meaning from marks, vestiges, and scratches.   L.

PLATE 36.

DECORATIONS OF TWO WINDOWS AT THE SIDE OF
THE CATHEDRAL OF MONZA.

THESE two somewhat lofty and noble windows, with their remarkably rich and beautiful framework, give light to the sacristry of Monza Cathedral. The original plan may have been thus to decorate the entire court, but if so it was never carried out. The style is derived from the Lombard, but modified by the Bramantesque, and belongs to the very beginning of the sixteenth century. The architect is unknown. The framework is in a ruinous condition, having apparently been moulded of an inferior clay, which is highly granular, and may have contained much earthy and organic matter.

L.

THE SANCTUARY OF CREMA, CALLED SANTA MARIA DELLA CROCE.

SCALE OF PLATE 38.

THIS building was erected between 1490 and 1500, and is the work of Giovanni Battista Battagli, an architect of Lodi. It belongs to the period of Greco-Roman or classic revival, which I mentioned when writing of the campanile of San Rustico, Caravaggio; and its simple design is very happily conceived. The lower portion, which surrounds the internal drum, whereon the cupola is based, is Bramantesque, or of the Cinquecento. The drum, which sustains the great cupola, shows something of the Lombard style; a variation attributable, as I think, not to accident but to design, and which serves in fact to distinguish the central portion from its adjuncts, making of it one complete feature, each order of architecture giving saliency to the other. The Bramantesque (for by what other name shall we call it?) is the simplest style imaginable; in which architecture constitutes the decoration of the architecture itself, although there are also certain minute carvings not discernible from a distance. Thus in the church we are considering, the projections serve as antechambers whereby to approach the shrine, whilst the quasi temples aloft with their small cupolas answer no purpose beyond that of ornament.

The classic school revived by Bramante was regarded as an innovation by many architects of that day, who adhered to their accustomed style of design,

Q

even in buildings erected later than 1500. Others adopted the new style exclusively. Others, again, had skill enough to profit by both schools; and amongst these last must be reckoned the architect Battagli, as is proved to us by this very shrine of Santa Maria della Croce.

This building bears out my observation, that the more recent brick is of a deeper shade of red than the ancient. Such later bricks are more liable to atmospheric oxidation; and on an oxidised surface dust and mud effect an easy lodgment, so that in time an entire edifice assumes an earthy-brown or dark-brown tint. Thus the encroachments of damp and wet are encouraged, which pave the way to the action of frost; finally, the material itself gives way; and thus it is that many comparatively modern buildings, amongst which must be included Santa Maria della Croce, present an aspect of greater age than their ancient predecessors.

L.

PLATE 39.

THIS house, which belongs to the beginning of the sixteenth century, stands opposite the church of the Carmine, and only two sides of its cortile remain. The figures, carvings, and terra-cotta ornaments, all carefully carried out with a certain pedantic conceit, are of a dark-red colour. Our artist found the walls dirty and ill-conditioned, and the paintings scarcely recognisable; yet under the pretty little portico, especially on the cross-lunettes of the vaulting, certain charming and delicate ornaments in chiaroscuro, with here and there a fillet or background of colour, remain in good preservation.

L.

Upper part of a private house at Pavia

PLATE 40.

THIS house is now a mere ruin : the Plate represents it after an imaginary process of restoration, by which the fragments of the four sides have been combined to form a sort of whole. This house stands in one of the streets situated between the church of the Carmine and the cathedral.   L.

PLATE 41.

SCALE OF PLATE 41.

THIS palace, abandoned and neglected for centuries, is now occupied by the steward and some inhabitants of the village and environs of Abbiate Grasso. In days of yore it served as a summer residence for some of the later Dukes of Milan, especially when hunting in the neighbouring woods of the Ticino. The few terra-cotta cornices now to be seen are clumsily modelled and put together, whilst the frescoes display a certain amount of painstaking, and are executed in very bright colours; amongst which are a yellow and a green, finer than any we now possess. The thin lines marked on the walls for the friezes, &c., are simply scratches made on the lime when freshly laid and still wet, and are rudely and irregularly done. All show that whilst a competent artist designed the decorations, their execution was left to inexperienced youths or mere workmen.

L.

PLATE 42.

ELEVATION OF A HOUSE IN PAVIA, NEAR THE HOSPITAL.

PAVIA, once capital of the Longobardic kingdom, subsequently the residence of several Dukes of Milan, became in consequence not only the head-quarters of persons attached to the court, or occupying official positions, but also of the noblest and most honourable families. Hence Pavia, beyond many of its sister cities, is rich in remains of old houses, one of these ruinous dwellings forming the subject of our present Plate. The windows, carefully executed in terra-cotta, are well preserved; but the paintings, with even such incisings as traced foliage and ornaments, have almost utterly vanished, not only through the agency of time, but yet more it may be by reason of repeated whitewashings. The coat of whitewash, originally perhaps clumsily laid on, has in its turn in great part peeled off the walls, and thus a clear field remains on which a discriminating and expert eye, aided by an ingenious guess, may track out the original design.

L.

A window in a private house at Pisa

PLATE 43.

WINDOW OF A PRIVATE HOUSE, IN PAVIA.

ERECTED in a side street to the left, but visible from the Corso Ticino as you pass beyond the University, stands this window, of rather large size and much broken. The painting of the small columns of the upper cornice, and a fragment or two below the window, are brightly coloured and distinct; all else is lost, thanks to repeated restorations of the fabric of the wall. The incised work has been traced out on a remote angle of the house, abutting on the neighbouring Contradella.

PLATE 44.

CASA ARCIMBOLDI, NOW BUSCA, NEAR MILAN

SCALE OF PLATE 44

VEN to the present day this great country house has retained its lordly aspect, thanks to the plan and structure of the house itself, of the spacious cortile by which it is approached, of the wall of enclosure which surrounds cortile, house, and garden alike, and of the two lodges which flank the entrance to the great cortile. It is now inhabited by a steward and his dependents. What few terra-cottas there are remain in good condition, but their ornamentation is too minute to be distinguishable, except on very close inspection. The paintings are all much defaced, yet some idea can be formed of them by bringing together such portions of the design as, because occupying sheltered situations, have suffered less by stress of weather. Our Plate represents the façade towards the court; that towards the garden is somewhat different. Above the apartments is built a superb tennis-court or open saloon, of which the wall that supports the roof is constructed with wide pilasters, between which stand two small arches supported by slender columns; thus the saloon is adequately decorated both within and without. There are no soffits. The beams which sustain the roof and constitute its decoration being adjusted with some elegance and well-shaped, produce an ornamental effect overhead; whilst the form of the roof, which rises highest at the centre, imparts to the whole a spacious and noble appearance. Within, the wall piers are rudely painted with niches, ornaments, and fillets of two colours; such

T

painted niches being occupied sometimes by a warrior, sometimes by a mythological demigod, and sometimes by a lady in the costume of the fifteenth century. The wall of the parapet is painted on the inside with a palisade of twisted osiers enclosing flowering shrubs. This saloon or tennis-court must have been appropriated to fencing matches, to gymnastic exercises, and to games.

L.

a. Tiled panel from an ancient villa at ... Foot of the Madonna del ... near Venice
b. Similar decoration from an ancient villa at ... south ... near

PLATE 45.

THE frequency with which 1487 is marked upon this wall indicates the date when it was either built or painted; the objects pourtrayed upon it express the aristocratic ostentation of the period. Most prominently, and on a somewhat large scale, appear the armorial bearings of the family who owned the villa, with other shields, perhaps those of their wives and near kindred, whilst the prevailing hue of fillets, rhombs, and squares records the colour of the political party to which they adhered. Rural objects are also represented there,—birds, flowers, fruits, in bright strong colours, which may even be over-bright, yet harmonise well with the mass of tree-foliage which surrounds that portion of the house. On high are seen nooks prepared for pigeons or other birds to build in, and certain yellow cross-markings are perhaps intended to suggest the idea of beehives. On the ground-floor there may have been the chapel or family oratory; the special purpose to which this portion of the house was dedicated being perhaps shown by a wall-painting of the Madonna with the Holy Child and S. Joseph, and by religious symbols introduced amongst the window decorations. Some of the paintings are rudely executed, some carefully. The idea of embellishing a country house with representations of cheerful objects, such as recall rural pleasures, is decidedly good.

b. UPPER PART OF AN OLD COUNTRY HOUSE AT UBALDO, NEAR SARONNO.

THIS house, surmounted by the characteristic Italian battlements, seen also in the preceding example, is approached through an excessively dirty and ill-kept peasants' court, and is itself occupied by peasants.   L.

PLATE 46.

WINDOW OF A COUNTRY HOUSE, NEAR MILAN.

Scale
of
Plate 46.   15   30   Mètres.

English feet.

AN hour's walk out of Milan, through Porta Nuova and Porta Comasina, brings one to this house, now occupied by peasants exclusively. It is a very dilapidated building, and none but a practised eye can detect in it aught worthy of note.

L.

Portion of a private house at Broussa

PLATE 47.

PART OF A PRIVATE HOUSE, IN BRESCIA.

Scale
of
Plate 47.

Mètres.

English feet.

THIS decorative fragment marks a house in one of those streets which lead from the Corso di Porta Torrelonga up to the Castle. It is a small unattractive fragment; in fact, a combination of various details here and there traceable on the ruinous wall.

L.

www.ingramcontent.com/pod-product-compliance
Lightning Source LLC
Chambersburg PA
CBHW031113020726
47495CB00007B/2178